Beans

Terry Jennings

Photographs by Ed Barber

Contents

A & C Black · London

Eating beans

Do you like beans?

How many different bean dishes have you tasted?

I'm eating beans in their pods.

Runner beans

Chilli con carne

Baked beans on toast

Sweet bean cakes

Spring roll

A CIP catalogue record for this book
is available from the British Library.

ISBN 0–7136–3220–8

A & C Black (Publishers) Ltd
35 Bedford Row, London WC1R 4JH

Acknowledgements
Illustrations by Lorraine Harrison (inside);
Katherine Greenwood (back cover and title-page)
Photographs by Ed Barber, except for: pp 4 (middle), 13 (bottom) Barrie Watts;
p 14 (top) FMC Corporation (UK) Limited; p 14 (bottom) Bedfordshire Growers Limited;
p 15 Maggie Murray/Format.

The author and publisher would like to thank the following people
whose help and co-operation made this book possible:
The staff and pupils of Brecknock Primary School; Peter Lavis and the staff of the
canning factory, Nestle Company Limited; Mihoko Tanaka.

Typeset by August Filmsetting, Haydock, St Helens
Printed in Belgium by Proost International Book Production

You may even have eaten beans without recognising them.

What are beans?

Beans are seeds which grow in pods. There can be as many as eight beans in a pod, or there can be just one. Bean pods grow on bean plants.

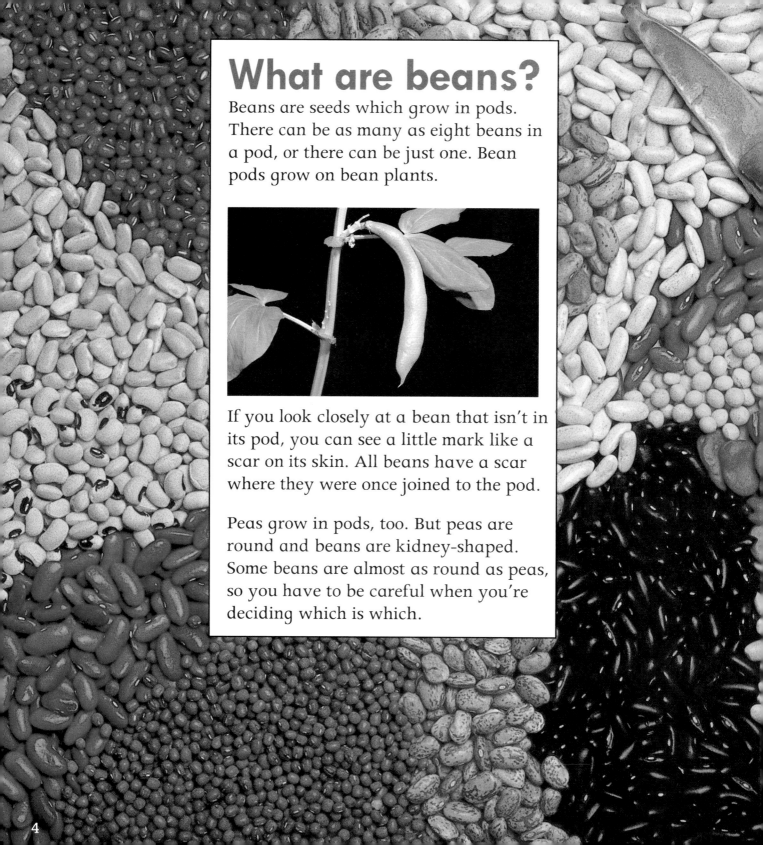

If you look closely at a bean that isn't in its pod, you can see a little mark like a scar on its skin. All beans have a scar where they were once joined to the pod.

Peas grow in pods, too. But peas are round and beans are kidney-shaped. Some beans are almost as round as peas, so you have to be careful when you're deciding which is which.

Dried, canned, frozen or fresh

Go to a health food shop and look at packets of dried beans. What different kinds can you find?

You can find frozen beans and canned beans in a supermarket. What different kinds are there? Are there any kinds that are canned as well as dried, or both canned and frozen? Make a chart to show what you have found.

In summer, you can see fresh beans at a greengrocer's. What kinds is the grocer selling? Ask where they came from. Ask which months are best for buying fresh beans, and which sort of bean is the first to come into the shops each year.

Make a collection of different beans, including, if possible, dried, canned, frozen and fresh beans. If some are in pods, take them out. (This is called shelling them.)

Measure how long and how wide your beans are. Then count out thirty of each kind, and weigh them. Which beans are the heaviest?

What difference can you see between the skin of a fresh bean and the skin of a frozen one? Try squashing different beans between your finger and thumb. Which are the softest – canned, dried or fresh beans? Dried beans have to be soaked before they are soft enough for cooking.

6

You could try soaking some dried beans. Quarter-fill a jam jar with the beans. Pour in water until the jar is three-quarters full. Leave the beans soaking overnight.

Next day, what has happened? Are the beans bigger or smaller than they were before? Are they heavier or lighter? Softer or harder? Why do you think they've changed so much? They even smell different now.

Dried beans always have to be soaked before they're cooked – but never eat them till after cooking. Some beans are poisonous unless they've been boiled for at least fifteen minutes.

Inside a bean

What do you think is inside a bean? If you've managed to buy fresh beans, split one in half with your fingernail. Otherwise, split open one of the dried beans that you've already soaked in water. (*Page 7*)

Inside every bean is a tiny bean plant. Can you see it? Can you see the root of the plant? Can you see a leaf? Which is bigger?

Most of your bean is filled with food for the little plant. The smooth, flat surfaces that you can see inside it are stores of food.

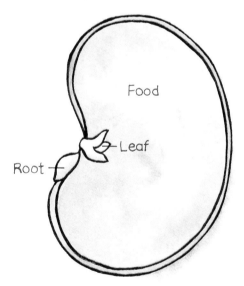

The bean plant is resting in the seed. It can stay this way for a long time. But when it does start to grow, it will use up the food around it.

8

Grow your own beans

You can watch bean
plants growing.

You will need

Paper towels
or blotting paper

Water

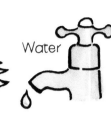

Canned
beans

4 jam jars

Frozen
beans

Fresh beans
(if possible)

Dried
beans

How to do it

Line the inside of each jar with some
curled-round blotting paper or three
paper towels folded together. Put about
2 cm of water into each jar. The paper
will soak up the water and become damp.

Slip four dried beans between the wet
paper and the glass of one of the jars.

Space out the beans all round the jar,
and try to position at least one with its
scar pointing upwards and one with its
scar downwards.

Put the other beans into the other jars,
then stand all the jars on a sunny
window-sill for four or five days.

9

Which of your beans grow? Which part grows first – the root or the shoot? Does it matter which way up the bean is?

Try to work out why some of the beans won't grow.

What does a bean need to make it grow well? Set up two more jam jars with dried beans in them, but only put water in one of them. Stand the jar without water on the window-sill as before. Put the jar with water in a fridge. Do the beans grow in either of the jars?

Bean sprouts for salad

Some kinds of bean are eaten as soon as they begin to sprout. You could try growing mung bean sprouts.

You will need

A dessertspoon of dried mung beans

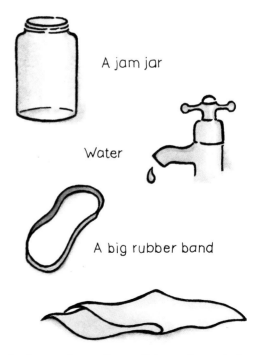

A jam jar

Water

A big rubber band

A piece of muslin or thin cotton cloth

How to do it

Half-fill the jar with water, and tip in the beans. Leave them soaking overnight. Then, with the rubber band, fix the cloth over the top of the jar and drain the water out through it. Leave the jar on its side in a warm, dark cupboard.

Twice a day, run fresh water on to the beans, through the cloth, and drain it all away again.

After a week, your beans should have sprouted. Try putting them in a salad with lettuce, cucumber, raw mushrooms and pineapple chunks.

Do your bean sprouts look different if you grow them in the light instead of in a dark cupboard?

11

Watching bean plants develop

If you want your beans to grow into more than just sprouts, you'll need to plant them in pots. Try growing some butter bean plants.

Put dried butter beans in large plant pots full of compost or fine soil. (Plant them about 3 cm below the surface.) Stand the pots on a tray on a sunny window-sill, and water the soil. From now on, make sure you keep it moist all the time.

Be patient! It may take a week for you to see any change. Don't disturb the pots – just keep watering and watching. What's the first thing you notice?

Measure how much your bean plants grow each week. Do they grow flowers?

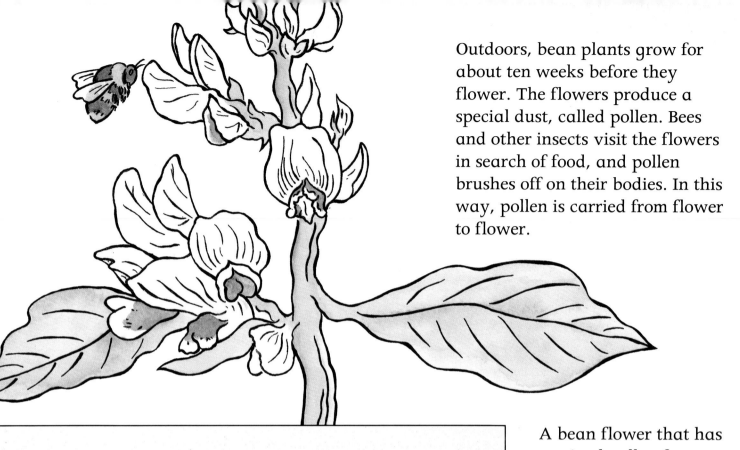

Outdoors, bean plants grow for about ten weeks before they flower. The flowers produce a special dust, called pollen. Bees and other insects visit the flowers in search of food, and pollen brushes off on their bodies. In this way, pollen is carried from flower to flower.

A bean flower that has received pollen from another flower of the same kind can start turning into a pod. As the pod grows, the flower petals die. The pod grows big, and the bean seeds inside ripen.

Gardeners and farmers grow beans out of doors, so it's easy for insects to visit the flowers. It takes about twelve weeks to grow mature bean plants with ripe pods.

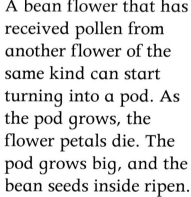

13

Farming beans

Beans are grown all over the world. Farmers like growing them because their roots contain tiny living things, called bacteria, that are good for the soil. You may have seen fields of broad or dwarf beans. When the plants have matured, the pods are picked by machine.

Runner beans grow up tall poles: their pods are picked by hand.

Some beans are grown as food for animals. Some are rushed to the shops, to be eaten fresh. Others are taken to factories, to be canned or frozen.

Beans for freezing first of all have to be cleaned. After that, they are passed into very hot water, then into cold water. Then they are quickly frozen solid and put into packets.

14

Most dried beans have come from hot countries, such as Tanzania, Ethiopia and parts of India and China. When the bean plants are full-grown, with ripe pods, they are cut down and left to dry in the sun. Then they can be brought in from the fields for sorting. The dried pods are easily split open, and the beans collected from them.

Drying, freezing and canning are all ways of stopping bacteria and fungi from growing on beans. As long as dried beans are kept dry, frozen beans kept frozen, and cans of beans kept unopened, they won't go bad.

Baked beans: the story

Canned baked beans have been around since 1875. They were first made in America. Have you ever wondered how today's baked beans are made?

Baked beans are really haricot beans, grown in North America and Canada. They are dried, and shipped to Britain in sacks.

In the baked beans factory, a worker slits open the sacks and tips the beans down a big funnel. Machines then sort them by size and colour. Any that are too small or dark end up in buckets, and will be sold as animal food.

Beans of the right size and colour are passed through tanks and pipes that wash them and partly cook them. They become softer.

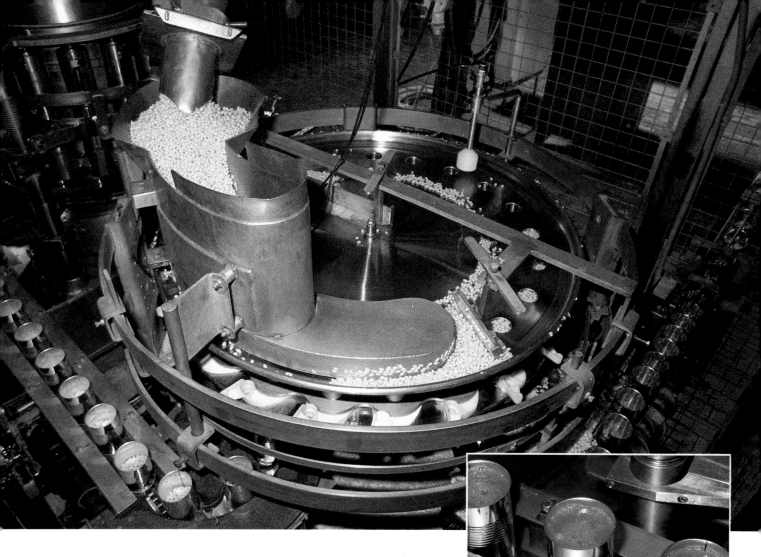

Then the beans are fed into a machine which drops them into cans. The machine releases exactly the right amount of beans into each can that comes along.

Another machine adds the tomato sauce, and then the cans have their lids sealed on. Finally, they are heated to 130°C, to kill any bacteria or fungi which might make the beans go bad. A machine sticks on the labels, and a factory worker gives the cans one last check. Then they're ready to be delivered to shops and supermarkets.

Make your own baked beans

The recipe for canned baked beans is a secret — but that doesn't mean you can't make your own baked beans. If you make them more than once, try adding different herbs and spices, to experiment with flavours.

You will need

150 g dried haricot beans

1 small onion finely chopped by an adult

6 pinches mustard powder

150 ml tomato juice

1 dessertspoon oil

1 tablespoon tomato purée

1 tsp brown sugar

2 tsp black treacle

Water for soaking

Equipment

Flameproof casserole with lid

Saucepan

Sieve

Cooker with oven and hot-plates or gas rings

Wooden spoon

How to do it

1. Tip your beans into the casserole and soak them in cold water overnight. Then drain them in the sieve and rinse them under a running tap.

Put your soaked beans into the saucepan with some water, and ask an adult to help you boil them gently on top of the cooker. Boil them for about an hour, adding more water when they need it. Then drain them.

2. Set the oven to 140°C (275°F) Gas Mark 1. Put the oil and the chopped onion into the casserole. Fry the onion on top of the cooker for about five minutes. Then stir in the beans and all the other ingredients, and bring the mixture to the boil. Put the lid on the casserole and put it in the oven.

3. Leave your beans to bake for about an hour. Then eat them with toast, naan, roti or pitta bread.

Make some sweet bean paste

Many bean dishes, such as baked beans, are savoury. But beans are used in sweet foods, too. In Japan and China, aduki beans are made into a paste for sweet fillings and little cakes.

You could make your own sweet bean paste. Eat it like jam – spread on bread or spooned into pastry tart cases.

You will need

Water

100 g sugar

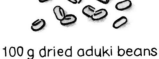
100 g dried aduki beans

Saucepan

Wooden spoon

Sieve

Bowl

Hot-plate or gas ring

How to do it

Put your beans into the bowl and soak them in water overnight. Then drain off the water through the sieve, rinse the beans and move them to the saucepan.

Pour water into the pan and put it on the hot-plate or gas ring. Bring the water to the boil.

Boil the beans for about two hours, adding more water to keep them always just covered. Then stir in the sugar.

Gently simmer the mixture – and stir occasionally – until the liquid is thick and syrupy. Then allow it to cool.

Delicious!

Beans for health

All beans contain vitamins and minerals which help to keep your body healthy. They also have a lot of dietary fibre in them, which is good for your digestive system. Fibre is too tough to digest, so it moves quickly through your body, carrying the body's waste products with it. It keeps the system working properly.

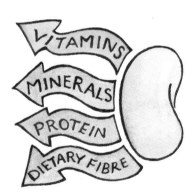

Beans contain lots of protein. You need protein to make your body grow. Protein also helps to replace body cells, such as blood cells and muscle cells, which wear out all the time.

Soya beans are the kind richest in protein. Lots of people eat them every day, especially in East Asian countries, such as China, Japan and Thailand. Soya beans can be made into curd (rather like soft cheese) or 'milk' or flour.

If you can get to a Chinese grocery shop, you could go and see bean curd (called tofu) being sold. How is it kept fresh?

Look for soya products in health food shops. Often, soya is disguised as something else: soya milk may be made into flavoured milk shakes, and soya flour processed so that, when cooked, it looks and tastes like meat.

Beans for celebrations

For seven or eight thousand years, people have been eating beans. The Ancient Greeks, Egyptians and Romans farmed them: the Greeks even had a god of beans, and held special bean feasts.

Today, beans are still an important part of people's lives – and not just as a food. In Japan, aduki beans are added to rice to colour it pinky-red. This rice, called seki-han, is eaten on happy occasions such as birthdays and weddings.

Tâoists eat mooncakes, filled with sweet, red bean paste, to celebrate the Mooncake Festival. They celebrate in September or October, when the moon is full. The cakes are round, like the moon, and have a special design pressed into the pastry on top.

More things to do

1. Collect different coloured dried beans and arrange them in a picture or pattern. You could make a collage by gluing your beans on to a piece of cardboard – or you could use them to decorate the outside of a shoe box. If you want your beans to look bright and shiny, paint them with clear varnish.

2. Make a maraca to shake by putting some dried beans in a plastic bottle or a yoghurt pot with a lid. Try to find out what is usually used as the outer casing for maracas. What kinds of beans are put inside?

3. You could use dried beans to make a bean-bag. Fold in half a rectangle of cotton cloth (about 12 cm × 22 cm) and sew up the sides, all except for one small gap. Use this gap to turn your bag inside-out, so that all the seams disappear inside. Fill the bag with dried beans – the more you put in, the less floppy your bean-bag will be. Finally, sew up the gap in the seam.

4. Make necklaces and bracelets by soaking dried beans until they're soft enough for you to stick a needle through the middle: put the beans on lengths of nylon thread. Make sure you dry them again, after threading them.

5. What happens if beans are left soaking in a jar of water for too long? Soak some dried beans overnight, and leave them in the same water all the next day. Do they begin to sprout? Leave them for another night and another day. Do they go on growing? What do they smell like? Flush the beans down the toilet after three days and nights of soaking. Apart from water and warmth, what do you think bean sprouts need to have, to make them grow well?

6. Beans come into quite a lot of sayings and expressions. Have you heard people say that someone is 'full of beans' – or that someone else 'hasn't got a bean'? What did they mean? What other bean sayings can you think of?

7. Some things are called beans although they're not real beans at all. Coffee beans aren't real beans; nor are jelly beans. Can you think of some more false beans?

Index

25